W9-BZT-229

KIMBERLY DERTING and SHELLI R. JOHANNES

Libby
LOVES SCIENCE

Illustrations by

JOELLE MURRAY

Greenwillow Books, An Imprint of HarperCollins Publishers

Libby loved science.
She loved mixing, pouring, measuring, and stirring.

Whipping up ingredients and making delicious things
to eat was one of Libby's favorite ways to experiment.

"Rainbow pancakes taste way better
than plain ones," she told her family.
And sometimes it was true!

At school, Libby's science teacher, Mr. Darwin, taught
the class about chemistry.
Libby loved chemistry because it is all about mixing,
pouring, measuring, and stirring.

"Not all chemical reactions occur at the same rate," said
  Mr. Darwin.
"Uh-oh," said Libby. "Looks like ours reacted too much!"
"Remember, your measurements need to be precise," said
  Mr. Darwin. "But it's okay—mistakes can lead to discoveries."
  And sometimes making mistakes was way more fun than
  cleaning up.

Foaming Fountain Experiment

MATERIALS:

* Safety goggles
* ½ cup 20-volume hydrogen peroxide liquid (20-volume is a 6% solution. Ask an adult to get this from a beauty supply store or hair salon.)
* A clean 16-ounce plastic bottle
* Food coloring
* Liquid dish soap
* Small cup
* 3 tablespoons of warm water
* 1 tablespoon (one packet) of dry yeast
* Funnel

Safety first!

INSTRUCTIONS:

1. Hydrogen peroxide can irritate skin and eyes, so put on those safety goggles and ask an adult to carefully pour the hydrogen peroxide into the bottle.
2. Add 8 drops of the food coloring to the bottle.
3. Add about 1 tablespoon of liquid dish soap and swish the liquid around a bit.
4. In a small cup, combine the warm water and the yeast and mix for about 30 seconds.
5. Pour the yeast-water mixture into the bottle (a funnel helps here) and watch the foaminess begin!

This experiment is sometimes called "Elephant's Toothpaste," because it looks like toothpaste coming out of a tube, but don't get the foam in your mouth!

NOTE: The foam will overflow, so be sure to do this experiment on a washable surface. ↑oops!

One day, Mr. Darwin made an important announcement.
"We are in charge of the science booth at our school's fall festival," he said.
Everyone was excited. The fall festival was fun, and Libby liked the science booth the best!

"Yay! We will have the best booth ever!" said Libby.
"This year, the booth that gets the most visitors and
collects the most tickets wins an ice cream party,"
said Mr. Darwin. "We need volunteers to run our booth."
Libby, Finn, and Rosa jumped up from their desks.
"We'll do it!" said Libby.

Libby, Finn, and Rosa met at Libby's house after school.
"We absolutely need to win," said Libby. "Just imagine . . .
an ice cream party!"
"I love ice cream!" said Rosa.

"Competing with the bouncy house won't be easy,"
said Finn.
"I think we can do really fun experiments that everyone
will want to try!" Libby said.
"Cool! We can decorate the booth, too," said Rosa.
"I have tons of art supplies," said Finn. "We can make
our booth really stand out."

Libby, Finn, and Rosa searched for fun experiments. They made a list of possibilities and voted for their three favorites.

Finn decided to make giant bubbles.

Rosa wanted to mix fluffy slime.

And Libby chose to launch a rocket.

"I can't wait for the festival!" she said.

Finally, the day of the festival arrived.
Libby, Finn, and Rosa got there early to
help Mr. Darwin set up the science booth.
Finn hauled in Hula-Hoops, dish soap, corn
syrup, and a kiddie pool.

Rosa carried a basket of shaving cream, glue, saline solution, and glitter.

Libby brought baking soda, vinegar, and empty water bottles.

They decorated the booth with posters, signs, and science stuff.

When the festival opened, the cotton candy booth
was swamped right away.
The dunk tank was a huge hit.
But the face-painting team was the one to beat.
The festival was crowded with friends and families
and teachers having fun.

"No one's coming to our booth!" said Finn.

"Maybe everyone thinks science is boring," said Rosa.

"Science is never boring," Libby said. "We just need to show them chemistry is fun!"

"I know," said Finn. "Let's blow some giant bubbles."
"The bigger, the better," said Rosa.
Finn filled the kiddie pool with water while Rosa
mixed in the soap.

"The secret ingredient is corn syrup," Libby said.
"Yup. It makes bubbles a bajillion times stronger!"
said Finn.

Giant Bubbles Experiment

MATERIALS:

* 6 cups distilled water (distilled water makes the best bubbles.)
* Large, clean container with lid
* 1 cup liquid dish soap (try to find a brand that doesn't say "Ultra")
* Glycerin or light corn syrup ⟶ secret ingredient! (shhh!)
* Bubble wand or straw (you pick the size)

INSTRUCTIONS:

1. Add the 6 cups of water into the container, then pour the dish soap into the water and stir slowly until the soap is mixed in. Try not to let foam or bubbles form while you stir.

2. Measure 1 tablespoon of glycerin or ¼ cup of corn syrup and add it to the container. Stir.

3. You can use the solution right away, but to make even better bubbles, put the lid on the container and let your super bubble solution sit overnight. ✦ ☽ ⚝

4. Dip a bubble wand or straw into the mixture, slowly pull it out, wait a few seconds, and then blow.

NOTE: If you used "Ultra" dish soap, double the amount of glycerin or corn syrup.

giant!

dish soap   water

"Next let's make some slime!" said Rosa to the small crowd that had gathered to make bubbles.
"Extra glitter equals extra sparkle," added Finn.

"It's important to add the saline . . . just a little at a time," said Libby.

"That's what makes it extra squishy!" said Rosa.

Fluffy Slime Experiment

MATERIALS:

* Gloves
* Container
* ⅔ cup of white glue
* ¼ cup water
* ½ teaspoon baking soda
* 2 to 3 cups shaving cream (gel)
* Glitter
* 1½ tablespoons saline solution (**Important:** the solution must have boric acid and sodium borate in the ingredients. This interacts with the glue to form the slime.)

INSTRUCTIONS:

1. Put on the gloves and add the glue to the container.
2. Add the water and baking soda and mix together.
3. Add the shaving cream.
4. Add the glitter.
5. Slowly stir in the saline solution, first 1 tablespoon then the remaining ½ tablespoon.

"Now for the grand finale!" said Rosa.

"Our rocket will be out of this world!" said Finn.

"We'll win for sure."

"If we use extra baking soda, the rocket might go even higher," said Libby.

"Science is a blast!" said Rosa.

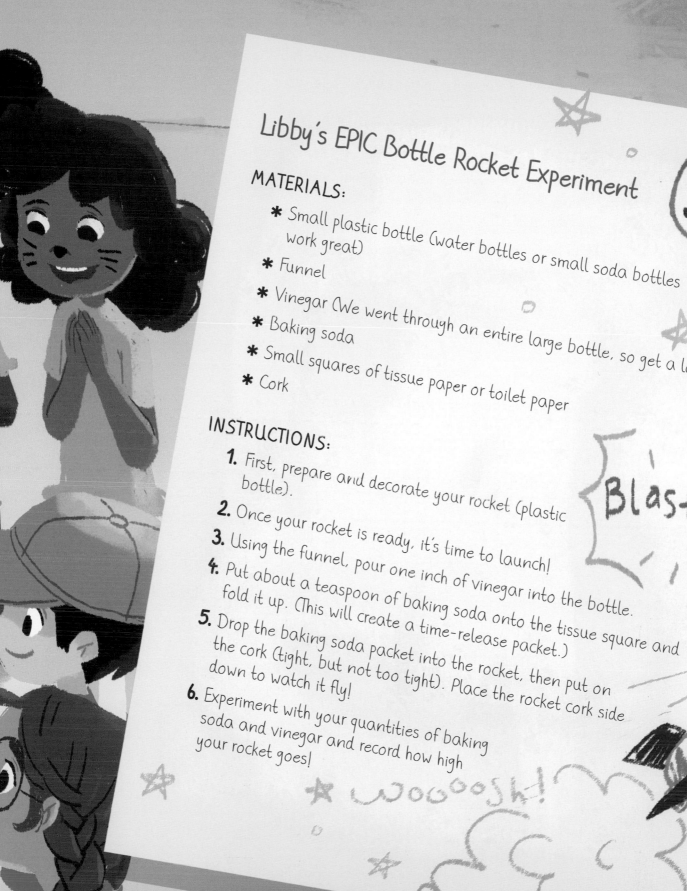

Libby's EPIC Bottle Rocket Experiment

MATERIALS:

* Small plastic bottle (water bottles or small soda bottles work great)
* Funnel
* Vinegar (We went through an entire large bottle, so get a lot!)
* Baking soda
* Small squares of tissue paper or toilet paper
* Cork

INSTRUCTIONS:

1. First, prepare and decorate your rocket (plastic bottle).
2. Once your rocket is ready, it's time to launch!
3. Using the funnel, pour one inch of vinegar into the bottle.
4. Put about a teaspoon of baking soda onto the tissue square and fold it up. (This will create a time-release packet.)
5. Drop the baking soda packet into the rocket, then put on the cork (tight, but not too tight). Place the rocket cork side down to watch it fly!
6. Experiment with your quantities of baking soda and vinegar and record how high your rocket goes!

Blast off

wooOOSh!

When Libby added in the baking soda, the liquid
started to bubble.
When the bottle filled up, the rocket zoomed high
into the air.
WHISSSSSSSSSSSSSSSSSSSSSSSHHHHH!

Unfortunately, it sprayed liquid everywhere. It sprayed all over the kids waiting in line. It sprayed way more than Libby predicted. Everyone got soaking wet and ran away.

"The face-painting booth still has a huge line," said Finn. "I don't think we have enough tickets."

"I'm sorry," said Libby. "I thought the rocket would be awesome."

"At least we got a big reaction," said Rosa.

The next day, Principal Neill announced the winner of the Fall Festival Booth Contest.

"The ice cream party goes to . . . the Art Club!" she said.

"Their face-painting booth won by a landslide."

Everyone cheered.

Even Libby, who felt she'd let her science class down.

Mr. Darwin called Libby, Finn, and Rosa to his desk. "You three did a great job on the booth!" he said.

"But we didn't win the ice cream party," mumbled Libby.

"That doesn't mean we can't celebrate how hard you tried," Mr. Darwin said. "Any ideas?"

"Maybe we can have our own party," Rosa said.

"What kind of party?" Finn asked.

"An ice cream party! And we can make our own ice cream!" Libby jumped up. "And I know exactly what we need."

Libby wrote a list of ingredients on the board.
Rosa borrowed sugar from the teacher's lounge.
Finn ran to the cafeteria for ice, vanilla, and milk.
Mr. Darwin grabbed rock salt and freezer bags from
his supply cabinet.

Ice Cream Experiment

MATERIALS:

* 1 tablespoon sugar
* ½ cup milk or ½ cup half-and-half
* ¼ teaspoon vanilla extract
* 1 sandwich zip-seal bag
* 2 tablespoons rock salt or 2 tablespoons table salt
* 1 gallon-sized zip-seal bag
* Lots of ice cubes
* Food coloring if you want a rainbow of ice cream!

INSTRUCTIONS:

1. Put the sugar, milk, and vanilla into the sandwich bag. Zip closed.
2. Place the rock salt in the gallon-sized bag and fill about ¾ full with ice cubes.
3. Place the sealed sandwich baggie in the larger bag and seal.
4. Take turns shaking and rolling the bag over and over until frozen (about 15 to 20 minutes).
5. Open and eat!

-milk
-Sugar
-ice cub

Libby walked the class through the steps in the recipe.
She even added lots of colors, because rainbow ice
cream usually tastes better than plain.

"This is delicious!" said Finn.

"Sometimes the best reactions aren't always the first reaction," Mr. Darwin said.

"Because ice cream is cool!" said Rosa.

"Yeah," said Libby, "and science is cool, too!"

Libby's Science Facts

- **Charles Darwin**—A scientist known for his theory of evolution—that animals change, or evolve, over time. He's also my science teacher, who often "experiments" with bow ties.

- **Chemistry**—The study of the properties of matter, and how matter interacts with energy. Every material in the universe is made up of matter— even our own bodies.

- **Chemical Reactions**—When things undergo a chemical change to form a different substance. For example, when you eat, your body uses chemical reactions to digest your food. Weird!

- **Experiment**—A scientific test done to see what happens to something under controlled conditions. I never do experiments without an adult's permission.

- **Measurements**—A number that shows the amount of something. For example, how many teaspoons of purple coloring to use in a pancake.

- **Observation**—The action of taking note of or viewing something.

- **Prediction**—A guess about what might happen. I *guessed* the rocket wouldn't spray water all over the crowd at the fair. Oops!

- **Science**—The study of the natural world through observation and experiments. Science is a blast!

To A. W. and J. D. for your undying support . . .
and for pretending to laugh at our jokes!—K. D. & S. R. J.

For both of my grandmas, Laura and Betty,
who instilled a love of learning within me,
and always encouraged curiosity.—J. M.

Libby says, "Experimenting with science is fun, but remember
that safety comes first, and always make sure a grown-up is there to help if you need it!"

Libby Loves Science
Text copyright © 2020 by Kimberly Derting and Shelli R. Johannes
Illustrations copyright © 2020 by Joelle Murray
All rights reserved. Manufactured in China. For information
address HarperCollins Children's Books, a division of
HarperCollins Publishers, 195 Broadway, New York, NY 10007.
www.harpercollinschildrens.com

The full-color art was created in Adobe Photoshop™.
The text type is Candida.

Library of Congress Cataloging-in-Publication Data

Names: Derting, Kimberly, author. | Johannes, Shelli R., author. | Murray, Joelle, illustrator.
Title: Libby loves science / written by Kimberly Derting and Shelli R. Johannes ;
    illustrated by Joelle Murray.
Description: First edition. | New York, NY : Greenwillow Books, an Imprint
    of HarperCollins Publishers, [2020] | Audience: Ages 4-8. | Audience: Grades 2-3. |
    Summary: Libby and her friends volunteer to run the science booth at their school
    fair and have some great ideas, but Libby does not always follow directions precisely.
    Includes a worksheet for each experiment mentioned.
Identifiers: LCCN 2019041788 | ISBN 9780062946041 (hardcover)
Subjects: CYAC: Science—Experiments—Fiction. | Science fairs—Fiction.
Classification: LCC PZ7.D4468 Lib 2020 | DDC [E]—dc23
    LC record available at https://lccn.loc.gov/2019041788
21 22 23 24 SCP 10 9 8 7 6 5 4 3 2
First Edition
Greenwillow Books